The battle in England!

The quarrel in Byzantium!

My second scar from Jorvik!

The accident at the summer party!

For Björn Desmond Manning with our love

What a Viking! *was made on location in Sweden and England in 1999.*
Thanks to: Lars Holmblad at The National History Museum, Stockholm,
Kristina Granström, Marit and Bosse, Olav Trätelja, Odin, Thor, Frey and Freya,
Sigtuna Museum, Birka, Jorvik Museum – and the island of Lindisfarne.

Consultant: Lars Holmblad, National History Museum, Stockholm

Rabén & Sjögren Bokförlag, Stockholm
http://www.raben.se

Originally published in Sweden by Rabén & Sjögren Bokförlag
under the title *Vilken viking!*, text and illustrations copyright © 2000
by Mick Manning & Brita Granström
Library of Congress catalog card number: 00-024193
Printed in Denmark 2000
First American edition, 2000
ISBN 91-29-64883-1

WHAT A VIKING!

MICK MANNING & BRITA GRANSTRÖM

R&S
BOOKS

Stockholm   New York   London   Adelaide   Toronto

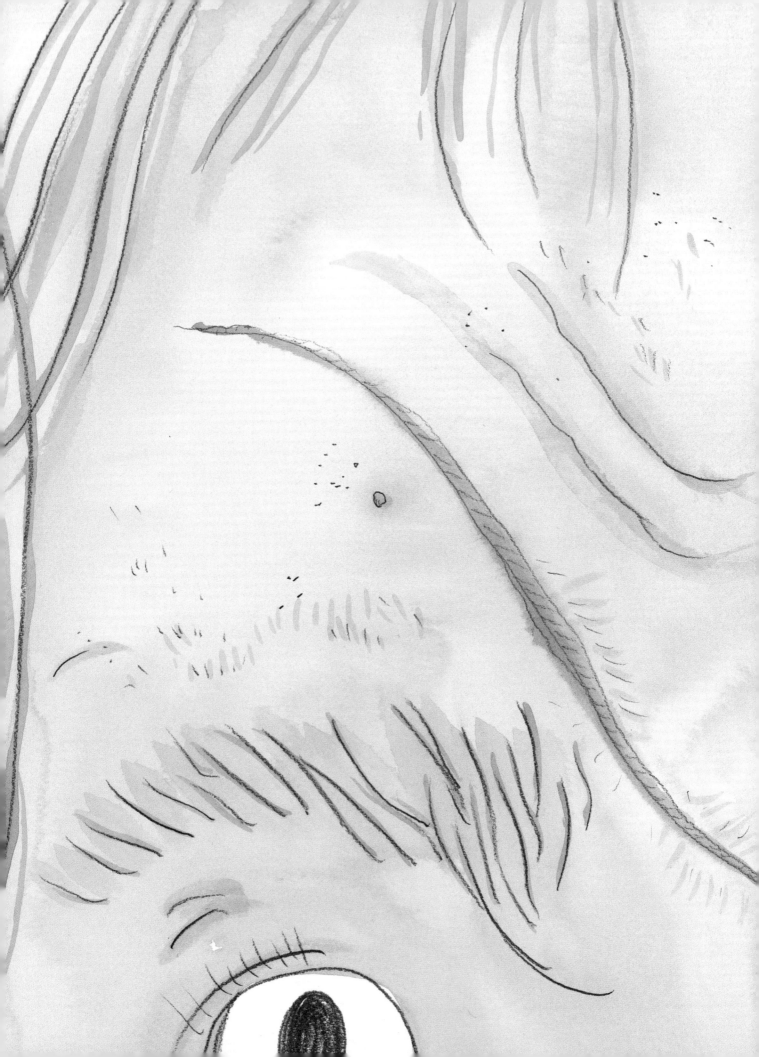

Look! What do you see?
Rivers winding through valleys?
Caves where dragons live?
Or a treasure map perhaps?
These are my scars . . .
my life story!

Here I am chop-chopping wood on a peaceful sunny day. But long ago I was a different sort of chopper ...

I was a Viking!

Vikings came from Sweden, Norway, and Denmark. They raided, explored, and settled in many other countries.

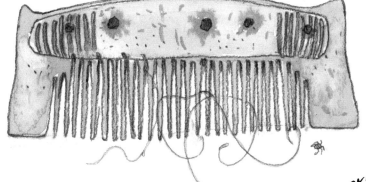

The English thought Vikings were very clean — they had a bath every Saturday and combed their hair!

I grew up in Birka — that was the busiest town in Sweden in those days. But by the age of thirteen I was bored!

I was fed up with being called "little Björn," fed up with unloading barrels of herring for my uncle, and fed up living at home with my bossy sister.

Viking keys hung from belts and chains.

Sails were made with the oily waterproof wool of Viking sheep.

Viking ships had oars for rowing into harbor or in case the wind dropped.

One morning I saw a wonderful sight …
gliding into the harbor like a golden eagle among the
sea gulls was a dragon-headed, red-and-white-
sailed sea serpent! How could a ship look so
beautiful? That very day I kissed my mother goodbye
and joined the crew — just like that!

Vikings had different sorts of boats: cargo boats, rowboats, and warships.

We sailed over the horizon and far away…
I had shipmates from Sweden, Denmark, and
Norway, and for a while our raiding adventures
became a way of life for us. I grew taller, stronger,
and uglier every year! I wasn't "little" Björn any
more! I loved the smell of the sea and the wind
on my hairy young face.

Vikings slept in
oilskin sleeping bags.
Some even had
feather-filled
quilts.

Vikings kept their things in the chests they sat on or under the deck.

A Viking tool chest

At sea, Vikings ate dried fish, meat, fruit, oats, and hard bread.

I helped burn down a few churches — and I stole my share of silver, too! Like many other Vikings, I didn't know any better in those days. We had a whole team of gods to help us ... Odin, the one-eyed wizard, Thor, who killed giants with a magic hammer, Frey and Freya, who made both our crops and babies grow! Tyr, the god of war, and the Valkyrie maidens, who carried Viking heroes to Valhalla ... Oh, and let's not forget Loki — he was always up to no good.

Vikings chopped up their treasure so they could share it.

Bitsilver

Vikings wore symbols of their favorite gods. Some wore christian crosses, too — the more gods the better. that's how they saw it!

viking cross

Odin's spear

Two Thor's hammers

Frey's steel

cross from England found in Sweden

Bitsilver was often made into new jewelry, like this snake ...

A comb from Byzantium

A bronze flask brought home to Sweden

We didn't always stay with the same ship. One year I joined a ship sailing east. We sailed across monster-infested seas and rowed down winding rivers until we reached a faraway city called Byzantium. What sweet memories that word brings back! I got into some adventures there; in fact it was where I got my first scar …

Arab coins were often taken home and used as jewelry.

After a year or two living in Byzantium, I sailed west to
Dublin. What a town! Shiploads of silk and gold …

Markets full of leather workers, shoemakers,
comb makers, jewelers — and slave traders …

I got a proper job in Dublin — as a bodyguard
for the Earl of Orkney's kids, Tovi and Toki.

You might call that babysitting, — but this
babysitter carried his ax at all times!

You could buy all these things in Viking Dublin...

bone ice skates

leather shoes

wooden toys

a ring pin for your cloak

or amber beads

A Viking toilet was a deep hole in the ground with a seat on top.

Viking poop found in Dublin

Tweezers and ear scoop found down a Viking toilet

Many Vikings had tummy bugs because their toilets leaked into their drinking water!

And I soon had to use it! I'd only left the kids for a minute — even Vikings have to use the toilet! When I got back, a slave trader had grabbed them. He was a big bully dressed in sealskin, and he claimed I had to either pay him or fight to get the kids back … So, guess what I did? "Fish breath" was more used to whipping slaves than fighting. He didn't last long. I got a scar for my trouble and my reputation as the best bodyguard money could buy! Oh yes, I set all his slaves free as well …

Viking duels were fought on a cloak. If you stepped off or lost the fight, the winner got all your property!

The stars at night and this sun compass found in Greenland helped the Vikings discover America a thousand years ago.

This Viking pin was found in America.

One spring a crowd of us set sail for new adventures. Some ships sailed north to Scotland and Iceland; others sailed home to Scandinavia …

Me? I sailed to join Olaf's army — we were going to conquer England!

A few weeks later I had survived a battle!
Hundreds of people fighting and shouting and chopping
at each other. We won, but my head got split wide open
by a sword cut. That's how I got my third scar.

A Viking's favorite weapons...

spear

battle ax

sword

arrow

skulls found in
England show how
Vikings died in
battle...

Smiths made tools and weapons – and some made jewelry. If a smith burned his hand, he plunged it into a bucket of pee – it was a sort of antiseptic!

Jorvik was the center of Viking England. Lots of
merchants and artists lived there — and robbers,
too, so I hired out my services as a bodyguard again.

One night I was guarding a moneylender when we got
ambushed by two "cutthroats." With a couple of blows,
I knocked one of them unconscions! But the second
was quick as a snake. First he slashed my face, then he
stabbed my arm! My blood began to flow like water
from a leaky barrel! Luckily, he slipped in the mud, and
we made our escape in the moonlight.

A few years later I met Thora. She was the
village stone-lifting champion — and when
she started sending me love letters carved in
runes, I knew I'd met my match! We soon
settled down together, and like lots of old
Vikings I became a farmer.

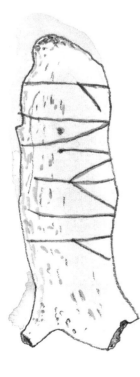

← The runes on this bone say "Kiss me!"

Vikings didn't use forks — just their own knife and sometimes a wooden spoon.

Vikings were good farmers and they loved feasts!

All Vikings like parties, and that's where I got my
sixth scar — at a midsummer festival.

There was wrestling, ax-throwing, stone-lifting,
games for the kids … But even Vikings can have
accidents, and during the archery contest someone
missed the target and I got the silly donkey's arrow
stuck in my hairy backside!

Vikings loved summer sports. In the winter they played board games and told stories about their gods and heroes.

← This chess piece was found on a Scottish island.

Viking sweets!

Dried apple rings

Aniseed pods

Pine tree resin "chewing gum"

So, now that you've heard my story, take another look at my scars — what do you see? Rivers winding through valleys? Caves where dragons live? Or a treasure map, perhaps …

Dogs, cats, hawks, and ferrets were common Viking pets – they were useful for hunting, too!

Helpful words

Art — Vikings were great artists, carving stone and wood and making jewelry, shoes, clothing, and everyday objects, like combs, in their own "Viking style."

Byzantium — Capital of the vast Byzantine Empire in the Middle East. Byzantium, also known as Constantinople, is now called Istanbul. Some Vikings worked there guarding the Emperor.

Combs — were important not just to look tidy but to get rid of lice and nits, common pests in hair and beards!

Cutthroat — A name for a robber.

Dublin — An important Viking-Age market town. A Viking longship found at Roskilde in Denmark was originally built in Dublin.

Ear scoop — Vikings cleaned their ears and kept the wax to use as a moisturizer for chapped hands in the winter!

Frey and Freya — Viking gods who made the seasons come and go. They also made all living things grow.

Jorvik — The most important town in Viking-Age England. Now it's called York.

Language — The Vikings took their Old Norse language with them wherever they settled. Many everyday English words, like *knife, egg, window, want, ill, die,* come from the Vikings.

Odin — The most powerful Viking god, who swapped an eye for magic powers. His ravens, Hugin and Munin, told him all that went on in the world — past, present, and future.

Runes — Viking letters that could be easily carved on wood, stone, or bone.

Slaves — People sold by force to be the property of someone else. No one wanted to be made a slave — the Viking name Karl actually means "free man."

Thor — The Vikings' favorite god. He rode in a chariot pulled by goats, and made thunder.

Tummy bugs — Dirty drinking water can spread diseases as well as parasites like roundworms. Vikings might have had a bath every week — but like everyone else they had bugs living in their tummy and nits in their hair.

Valhalla — Odin's feasting hall. Half the Vikings who died in battle went there — the others went to Frey and Freya's place.

Vikings — started as the word for sea raiders but soon became a name for all the people who came from Sweden, Denmark, and Norway at that time. Vikings later settled in other countries, including Scotland, Ireland, England, Iceland, Greenland, France, Russia, and even America for a short time.

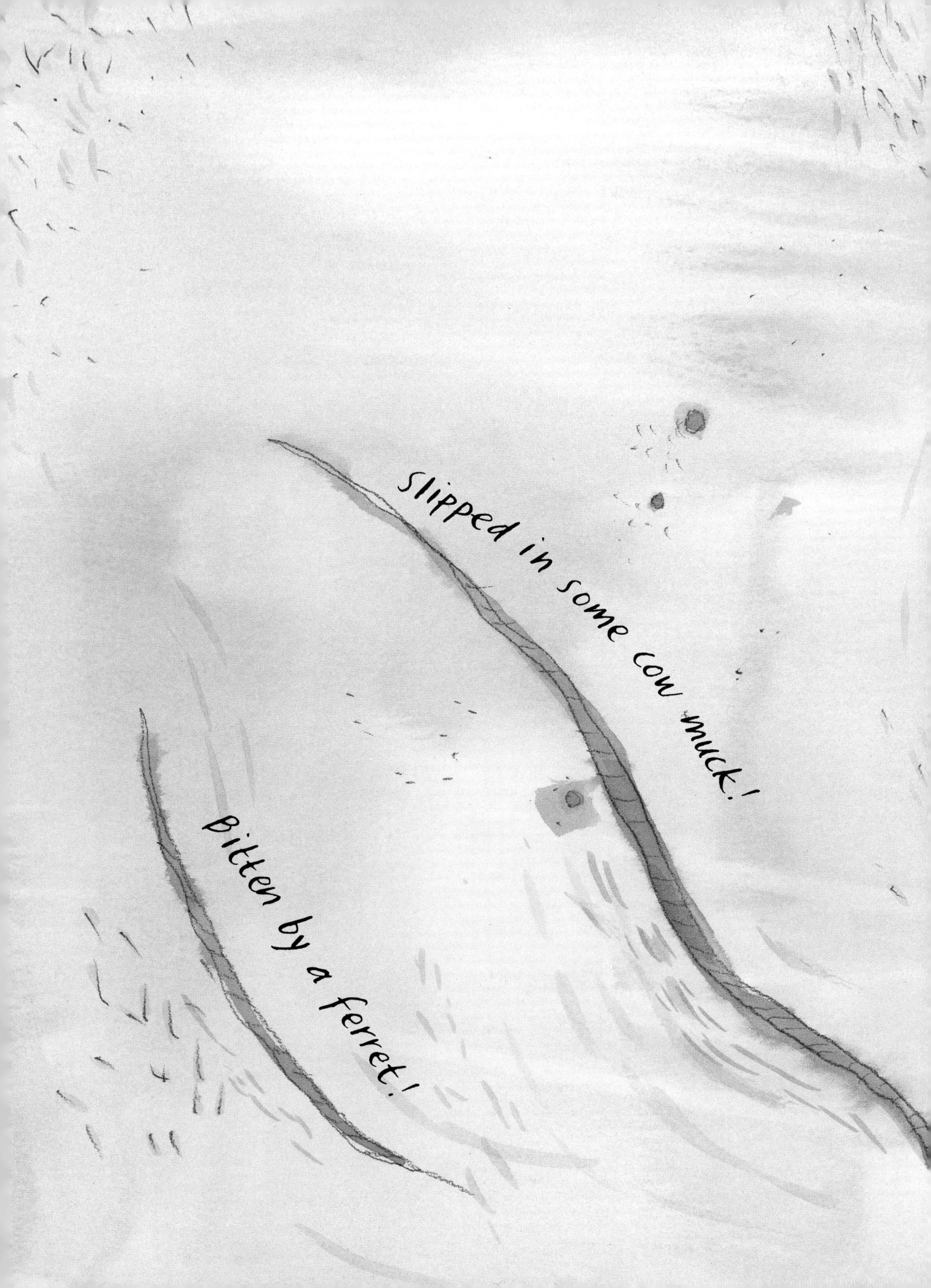
Slipped in some cow muck!
Bitten by a ferret!